Contents

About *ISSUES* today

ISSUES today is a series of resource books on contemporary social issues, designed for Key Stage 3 pupils and above. This series is also suitable for Scottish P7, S1 and S2 students.

Each volume contains information from a variety of sources, including government reports and statistics, newspaper and magazine articles, surveys and polls, academic research and literature from charities and lobby groups. The information has been tailored to an 11 to 14 age group; it has been rewritten and presented in a simple, straightforward and accessible format.

In addition, each **ISSUES** today title features handy tasks and assignments based on the information contained in the book, for use in class, for homework or as a revision aid.

ISSUES today can be used as a learning resource in a variety of Key Stage 3 subjects, including English, Science, History, Geography, PSHE, Citizenship, Sex and Relationships Education and Religious Education.

About this book

Understanding Stress is Volume 102 in the **ISSUES today** series.

One in five people regularly feel anxious and 20% of Brits have taken time off work due to stress. This book provides an in-depth look at stress and the effect it can have on everyday life. We ask if stress can be contagious, if there is such thing as 'good stress' and explore different anxiety disorders. *Understanding Stress* also considers different ways of managing stress, such as the use of colouring books and the importance of breathing properly.

Understanding Stress offers a useful overview of the many issues involved in this topic. However, at the end of each article is a URL for the relevant organisation's website, which can be visited by pupils who want to carry out further research.

Because the information in this book is gathered from a number of different sources, pupils should think about the origin of the text and critically evaluate the information that is presented. Does the source have a particular bias or agenda? Are you being presented with facts or opinions? Do you agree with the writer?

At the end of each chapter there are two pages of activities relating to the articles and issues raised in that chapter. The 'Brainstorm' questions can be done as a group or individually after reading the articles. This should prompt some ideas and lead on to further activities. Some suggestions for such activities are given under the headings 'Oral', 'Moral dilemmas', 'Research', 'Written' and 'Design' that follow the 'Brainstorm' questions.

For more information about **ISSUES** today and its sister series, **ISSUES** (for pupils aged 14 to 18), please visit the Independence website.

Stress

Stress is how you feel when the pressure you're under exceeds your ability to cope. Everyone reacts to stress differently. It can depend on your personality and how you respond to pressure.

Symptoms of stress

Everyone reacts to stress in different ways. However, there are some common symptoms to look out for. Your symptoms can be psychological (mental), emotional, behavioural or physical, or a mix of these.

Psychological symptoms of stress can include:

➤ constant worrying
➤ an inability to concentrate
➤ feeling that you have poor judgement
➤ seeing only the negative
➤ anxious thoughts
➤ memory problems.

If you're affected emotionally by stress, your symptoms may include:

➤ mood swings or changes in your mood
➤ irritability or having a short temper
➤ an inability to relax
➤ feeling overwhelmed
➤ a sense of loneliness
➤ depression
➤ low self-esteem.

Your behaviour might also change and you may be:

➤ eating more or less than usual
➤ sleeping too much or too little
➤ isolating yourself from others (being alone)
➤ neglecting or putting off responsibilities
➤ using alcohol, tobacco or illegal drugs to relax
➤ developing nervous habits; for example, nail biting or not being able to sit still.

Stress can affect you physically, causing symptoms such as:

➤ aches and pains
➤ diarrhoea and constipation
➤ nausea or dizziness
➤ chest pains
➤ loss of sex drive.

These symptoms may be caused by problems other than stress. If you have any of them, speak to your GP for advice.

If you have a pre-existing health condition, stress may cause it to worsen or flare-up. For example, conditions such as migraine, eczema, asthma, irritable bowel syndrome or psoriasis can all be made worse by stress.

Diagnosis of stress

There is no specific test to diagnose stress. If you think you're stressed or if you feel very anxious, talk to those around you who are likely to be supportive, or your GP. Your GP will usually be able to recognise the symptoms and give you advice about how to deal with it. Your GP may also suggest that you talk to a counsellor.

You might feel reluctant to ask for help if you're stressed or feel under pressure. But don't be afraid to speak to your GP, friends or family. It's important to recognise the symptoms of stress so you can learn how to manage them and begin to feel better.

One way of helping to identify your stress triggers, how you react to them and how they make you feel, is to keep a diary. You could make a note of what made you stressed, how stressed you became, what symptoms you experienced and how well you coped.

Treatment options for stress

There are a number of treatment options for stress. These are described on the next page. Which treatments you are offered will depend on your personal circumstances. Your GP will discuss these with you to help you make a decision that's right for you. Your decision will be based on your GP's expert opinion and your own personal values and preferences.

To be able to tackle stress, it's important to recognise the symptoms as well as the problems that it's causing. There are a number of ways to reduce the effect that stress can have on you. If these don't work, your GP may recommend other options, such as cognitive behavioural therapy (CBT).

Self-help

Exercise can be effective at relieving stress and is good for your wellbeing. It can improve your mood, give you a sense of achievement and help you release tension. According to the Department of Health, there's evidence that physical activity reduces your risk of depression and improves your quality of sleep. It helps reduce stress hormones and stimulates the release of endorphins (the hormones that make you feel good).

It can help to incorporate exercise into your daily routine. A brisk walk to the shops, cycling to work or gardening can help. The recommended healthy level of physical activity is 150 minutes (two-and-a-half-hours) of moderate exercise per week. One way to achieve this is to do 30 minutes of exercise at least five days a week.

There are a number of other things you can try to help deal with and manage your stress better.

- Manage your time more effectively and prioritise more important jobs first.
- Adopt a healthy lifestyle – eat a balanced diet, rich in fruit and vegetables, exercise regularly and make sure you get enough sleep.
- Know your limits – don't take on too much.
- Find out what causes you to feel stressed and try to change your thoughts and behaviour to reduce it – talking things over with a friend or a family member can help.
- Try not to get into situations that make you feel angry or upset.
- Accept the things you can't change and concentrate on the things you have control over.
- Make time for the activities you enjoy and for the things that make you feel relaxed – you're more likely to neglect this area of your life if you're stressed.
- Find time to meet friends and have fun – arrange to do something you enjoy.
- Develop a positive thinking style – try to look at a problem differently or discuss it with someone.
- Don't drink too much alcohol or caffeine, or use tobacco or illegal drugs as a way to cope. In the long term, these things will only make you feel worse.

You can also learn techniques to manage your stress from self-help books, podcasts and CDs, or by attending a stress management course. Some people find that meditative approaches, such as mindfulness, meditation, yoga or tai chi, are effective at reducing stress and anxiety. Yoga and tai chi help you control your breathing and relax your mind. Meditation helps you learn to reduce anxious thoughts and become calmer.

Explore the options available and find a solution that fits you, your lifestyle, work and personality. There is no right or wrong approach as everyone reacts to stress in different ways. And different approaches will work for different people.

Talking therapies

CBT is a talking treatment. It looks at how situations can lead to thoughts that impact your feelings and behaviour. It aims to change the way you think and behave, and helps you to challenge negative thoughts or feelings.

CBT can help to treat many problems, such as sleeping difficulties, relationship problems, drug and alcohol abuse, anxiety or depression. The therapy focuses on your thoughts, images, beliefs, feelings and attitudes (known as your cognitive processes) and how these relate to the way you behave. CBT sessions may be on a one-to-one basis or with a group of people. Sessions may last for between five and 20 weeks, with each session typically lasting between 30 and 60 minutes.

Medicines

Medicines are not generally helpful for treating stress.

Complementary therapies

Some people find that complementary therapies, including acupuncture, visualisation, reflexology and herbal remedies, offer some benefit. However, there isn't enough evidence to say if they are effective or not.

Massage and aromatherapy can promote a sense of wellbeing and provide a relaxing environment that helps you unwind. There's little scientific evidence to show whether or not aromatherapy is an effective treatment for stress.

You may find herbal remedies helpful, but it's important to remember that natural doesn't mean harmless. Herbal remedies contain active ingredients and may interact with other medicines or cause side-effects. Don't start taking any herbal remedies without speaking to your pharmacist first.

The above information is reprinted with kind permission from BUPA.
© BUPA 2015

www.bupa.co.uk

What is post-traumatic stress disorder?

If you are involved in or witness a traumatic event, it is common to experience upsetting, distressing or confusing feelings afterwards. The feelings of distress may not emerge straight away – you may just feel emotionally numb at first. After a while you may develop emotional and physical reactions, such as feeling easily upset or not being able to sleep.

This is understandable, and many people find that these symptoms disappear in a relatively short period of time. But if your problems last for longer than a month, or are very extreme, you may be given a diagnosis of post-traumatic stress disorder (PTSD).

There's no time limit on distress, and some people may not develop post-traumatic symptoms until many years after the event. Additionally, not everyone who has experienced a traumatic event develops PTSD.

Other terms for PTSD

The diagnosis 'PTSD' was first used by veterans of the Vietnam War, but the problem has existed for a lot longer and has had a variety of names, including:

➢ shell shock
➢ soldier's heart
➢ battle fatigue
➢ combat stress
➢ post-traumatic stress syndrome (PTSS).

Today, the term PTSD can be used to describe the psychological problems resulting from any traumatic event.

What are the symptoms?

The symptoms of PTSD can vary from person to person, although you may experience some of the following.

Reliving aspects of the trauma:

➢ vivid flashbacks (feeling that the trauma is happening all over again)
➢ intrusive (unwelcome/disruptive) thoughts and images
➢ nightmares
➢ intense distress at real or symbolic reminders of the trauma
➢ physical sensations, such as pain, sweating, nausea or trembling.

Alertness or feeling on edge:

➢ panicking when reminded of the trauma
➢ being easily upset or angry
➢ extreme alertness
➢ a lack of or disturbed sleep
➢ irritability and aggressive behaviour
➢ lack of concentration
➢ being easily startled
➢ self-destructive behaviour or recklessness.

Avoiding feelings or memories:

➢ keeping busy
➢ avoiding situations that remind you of the trauma
➢ repressing memories (being unable to remember aspects of the event)
➢ feeling detached, cut off and emotionally numb
➢ being unable to express affection
➢ using alcohol or drugs to avoid memories.

You may also develop other mental health problems, such as:

➢ severe anxiety
➢ a phobia
➢ depression
➢ a dissociative disorder
➢ suicidal feelings.

MUST KEEP BUSY!

What causes PTSD?

The situations we find traumatic can vary from person to person and different events can lead to PTSD. It may be that your responses have been bottled up for a long time after the traumatic event has passed. Your problems may only emerge months or sometimes years after a traumatic experience, affecting your ability to lead your life as you'd like to.

A traumatic event could include:

- a serious accident, for example a car crash
- an event where you fear for your life
- being physically assaulted
- being raped or sexually assaulted
- abuse in childhood
- a traumatic childbirth, either as a mother or a partner witnessing a traumatic birth
- extreme violence or war
- military combat
- seeing people hurt or killed
- a natural disaster, such as flooding or an earthquake
- losing someone close to you in disturbing circumstances.

The following factors may also make you more vulnerable to developing PTSD after experiencing a traumatic event, or might make the problems you experience more severe:

- experiencing repeated trauma
- getting physically hurt or feeling pain
- having little or no support from friends, family or professionals
- dealing with extra stress at the same time, such as bereavement or loss
- previously experiencing anxiety or depression.

Anyone can experience a traumatic event, but you may be more likely to have experienced one if you:

- work in a high-risk occupation, such as the police or military
- are a refugee or asylum seeker
- have suffered childhood abuse.

Different types of trauma can have different types of impact. If you experienced trauma at an early age or if the trauma went on for a long time then you may be diagnosed with 'complex PTSD'. Treating 'complex PTSD' usually requires more long-term, intensive help than supporting you to recover from a one-off traumatic event.

The above information is reprinted with kind permission from Mind.
© Mind 2015

www.mind.org.uk

Is stress contagious?

Exams looming, a large unexpected bill, tension at work? These don't have to be your problems for your health to be affected by them.

redefining / standards

We all know what it's like to feel stressed. But many of us also have to deal with the impact of stress on those close to us. And this second-hand stress can have a dramatic effect on our lives.

Are you at risk?

Psychology Professor Elaine Hatfield of the University of Hawaii, and others, have carried out research in this area and developed the theory that, along with other feelings and emotions, stress is contagious – something we can catch from those around us.

Elaine explained there is an Emotional Contagion Scale – a set of 15 statements to measure susceptibility to 'catching' other peoples' emotions. For instance, if you answer 'always', to the statement 'I tense when overhearing an angry quarrel' you're likely to be more at risk to emotional contagion than someone who answers 'never'.

Synchronised emotions

Researchers believe emotional contagion can happen when we imitate people's facial expressions, vocal sounds, language and posture, often without realising it. For example, if someone smiles at you, often you smile back, and may feel happier because of this.

As a result of this mimicry we are more likely to synchronise with other people, and pick up on their feelings. The good news is that emotional contagion applies to more positive feelings as well, such as happiness.

Consequences of stress

Experts in this field believe emotional contagion affects groups as well as individuals. Some believe it could be behind reports of mass hysteria.

But is the theory that we can 'catch' stress from others, as easily as a cold, generally accepted?

'We can't talk about stress in the same sense as a physical illness or disease,' says Dr Martin Bamber, Consultant Clinical Psychologist and founder of the York CBT Centre.

'However, when someone is stressed emotionally, they might be more irritable and short-tempered, perhaps feeling unwell and taking time off sick. And that can have consequences for those around them. Other people will be on the receiving end of the consequences of stress.'

The expert's opinion

'I think there is truth in this idea to a degree,' says Dr Nick Kambitsis of psychology consultancy Nicholson McBride. 'It depends on how the stress manifests itself in the individual.'

'If they become snappy and irritable, don't listen and don't engage with other people, I agree it can be contagious, because it will have an impact on people around them. But not everyone responds to stress in this way. Some withdraw, and some stay calm and consistent.'

Stress and your health

Stress, at the right time and place, can be useful. A sudden surge of hormones when you need it can make the difference between catching the bus or missing it – or winning the match or losing.

However, long-term stress – when you're under more pressure than you can cope with – can take its toll on your health. And that's a good reason to avoid stress if you can.

Symptoms such as headaches, trouble sleeping and being unable to concentrate can be a result of stress. Other, longer-term problems include blood sugar imbalance, increased abdominal fat and high blood pressure. These can lead to serious health problems, such as heart disease and stroke.

The Emotional Contagion Scale

The Emotional Contagion Scale is a 15-item index designed to measure how prone an individual is to 'catching' the emotions of others. It examines a person's tendency to mimic five basic emotions: sadness, fear, anger, happiness and love.

There are no right or wrong answers. Read each question and indicate the answer that best applies to you using the following key:

1 – Never   2 – Rarely   3 – Often   4 – Always

The higher the score, the more susceptible you are likely to be to emotional contagion.

1. If someone I'm talking with begins to cry, I get teary-eyed.
2. Being with a happy person picks me up when I'm feeling down.
3. When someone smiles warmly at me, I smile back and feel warm inside.
4. I get filled with sorrow when people talk about the death of their loved ones.
5. I clench my jaws and my shoulders get tight when I see the angry faces on the news.
6. When I look into the eyes of the one I love, my mind is filled with thoughts of romance.
7. It irritates me to be around angry people.
8. Watching the fearful faces of victims on the news makes me try to imagine how they might be feeling.
9. I melt when the one I love holds me close.
10. I tense when overhearing an angry quarrel.
11. Being around happy people fills my mind with happy thoughts.
12. I sense my body responding when the one I love touches me.
13. I notice myself getting tense when I'm around people who are stressed out.
14. I cry at sad movies.
15. Listening to the shrill screams of a terrified child in a dentist's waiting room makes me feel nervous.

Source: The Emotional Contagion Scale, Psychology Today, 2012.

Side-step your second-hand stress

Expert opinion points towards a knock-on effect of spending time with someone who is stressed. But you can take steps to reduce the effect their problems have on you.

Exercise. Exercise can be a good way to relieve stress. This is because it helps use up the hormones the body produces when under stress. It relaxes muscles, strengthens the heart, improves blood circulation and releases endorphins (chemicals that give a sense of wellbeing).

Use your brain and relax. Using your brain in a different way can help relieve stress. Listen to music, cook, read a favourite book – do something you enjoy and find relaxing.

Talk about it. Taking a more direct approach with the person causing your stress can help. 'Have a conversation with the family member or work colleague. Talk about the problem, and acknowledge that it exists,' says Dr Kambitsis.

'Often you can come up with strategies to deal with the problem. You may look at the past, and how they – and you – dealt with similar situations. Ask what you as a family or work team can do about the problem, what's going to make them feel better.' It should make you feel better too.

For more information on managing stress why not visit our Stress Centre (www.axappphealthcare.co.uk/health-information/mind-health/) where you will find features on 'stress proofing techniques' and 'managing pressure'.

www.axappphealthcare.co.uk

Mini glossary

Contagion – *something which is spread through close contact.*

Mimicry – *To mimic, copying.*

What are anxiety disorders?

There are various conditions (disorders) where anxiety is a main symptom. You may have an anxiety disorder if anxiety symptoms interfere with your normal day-to-day activities, or if worry about developing anxiety symptoms affects your life. About one in 20 people have an anxiety disorder at any one time. The following is a brief overview of the main anxiety disorders. Some people have features of more than one type of disorder.

Reactions to stress

Anxiety can be one of a number of symptoms as a reaction to stressful situations. There are three common types of reaction disorders:

Acute reaction to stress (sometimes called acute stress reaction)

Acute means the symptoms develop quickly, over minutes or hours, reacting to the stressful event. Acute reactions to stress typically occur after an unexpected life crisis such as an accident, bereavement, family problem, bad news, etc. Sometimes symptoms occur before a known situation which is difficult. This is called situational anxiety. This may occur, for example, before an examination, an important race, a concert performance, etc.

Symptoms usually settle fairly quickly, but can sometimes last for several days or weeks. Apart from anxiety, other symptoms include low mood, irritability, emotional ups and downs, poor sleep, poor concentration, wanting to be alone.

Adjustment reaction

This is similar to the above, but symptoms develop days or weeks after a stressful situation, as a reaction or adjustment to the problem. For example, as a reaction to a divorce or house move. Symptoms are similar to acute reaction to stress but may include depression. The symptoms tend to improve over a few weeks or so.

Post-traumatic stress disorder

Post-traumatic stress disorder (PTSD) may follow a severe trauma such as a serious assault or life-threatening accident. Symptoms last at least one month, often much longer. Anxiety is only one symptom which may come and go. The main symptoms of PTSD are:

➢ Recurring thoughts, memories, images, dreams, or flashbacks of the trauma, which are distressing.
➢ You try to avoid thoughts, feelings, conversations, places, people, activities or anything else which may trigger memories or thoughts of the trauma.

➢ Feeling emotionally numb and detached from others. You may find it difficult to have loving feelings.
➢ Your outlook for the future is often pessimistic. You may lose interest in activities which you used to enjoy.
➢ Increased arousal which you did not have before the trauma. This may include difficulty sleeping, being irritable, difficulty concentrating and increased vigilance.

Phobic anxiety disorders

A phobia is strong fear or dread of a thing or event. The fear is out of proportion to the reality of the situation. Coming near or into contact with the feared situation causes anxiety. Sometimes even thinking of the feared situation causes anxiety. Therefore, you end up avoiding the feared situation, which can restrict your life and may cause suffering.

Social anxiety disorder

Social anxiety disorder (also known as social phobia) is possibly the most common phobia. With social anxiety disorder you become very anxious about what other people may think of you, or how they may judge you. Therefore, you fear meeting people, or 'performing' in front of other people, especially strangers. You fear that you will act in an embarrassing way and that other people will think that you are stupid, inadequate, weak, foolish, crazy, etc. You avoid such situations as much as possible. If you go to the feared situation you become very anxious and distressed.

Agoraphobia

This too is common. Many people think that agoraphobia means a fear of public places and open spaces. But this is just part of it. If you have agoraphobia you tend to have a number of fears of various places and situations. So, for example, you may have a fear of:

- Entering shops, crowds and public places.
- Travelling in trains, buses or planes.
- Being on a bridge or in a lift.
- Being in a cinema, restaurant, etc., where there is no easy exit.

But they all stem from one underlying fear. That is, a fear of being in a place where help will not be available, or where you feel it may be difficult to escape to a safe place (usually to your home). When you are in a feared place you become very anxious and distressed, and have an intense desire to get out. To avoid this anxiety many people with agoraphobia stay inside their home for most or all of the time.

Other specific phobias

There are many other phobias of a specific thing or situation. For example:

- Fear of confined spaces or of being trapped (claustrophobia).
- Fear of certain animals.
- Fear of injections.
- Fear of vomiting.
- Fear of being alone.
- Fear of choking.

But there are many more.

Other anxiety disorders

Panic disorder

Panic disorder means that you get recurring panic attacks. A panic attack is a severe attack of anxiety and fear which occurs suddenly, often without warning, and for no apparent reason. The physical symptoms of anxiety during a panic attack can be severe and include a thumping heart (palpitations), trembling, feeling short of breath, chest pains, feeling faint, numbness or pins and needles. Each panic attack usually lasts five to ten minutes, but sometimes they come in waves for up to two hours.

Generalised anxiety disorder

If you have generalised anxiety disorder (GAD) you have a lot of anxiety (feeling fearful, worried and tense) on most days. The condition persists long-term. Some of the physical symptoms of anxiety (detailed above) may come and go. Your anxiety tends to be about various stresses at home or work, often about quite minor things. Sometimes you do not know why you are anxious. In addition, you will usually have three or more of the following symptoms:

- Feeling restless, on edge or 'keyed up' a lot of the time.
- Tiring easily.
- Difficulty concentrating and your mind going blank quite often.
- Being irritable a lot of the time.
- Muscle tension.
- Poor sleep (insomnia). Usually it is difficulty in getting off to sleep, or difficulty in staying asleep.

Mixed anxiety and depressive disorder

In some people, anxiety can be a symptom when you have depression. Other symptoms of depression include low mood, feelings of sadness, sleep problems, poor appetite, irritability, poor concentration, decreased sex drive, loss of energy, guilt feelings, headaches, aches, pains and palpitations. Treatment tends to be aimed mainly at easing depression and the anxiety symptoms often then ease too.

Obsessive-compulsive disorder

Obsessive-compulsive disorder (OCD) consists of recurring obsessions, compulsions, or both.

- Obsessions are recurring thoughts, images or urges that cause you anxiety or disgust. Common obsessions are fears about dirt, contamination, germs, disasters, violence, etc.
- Compulsions are thoughts or actions that you feel you must do or repeat. Usually a compulsion is a response to ease the anxiety caused by an obsession. A common example is repeated hand washing in response to the obsessional fear about dirt or germs. Other examples of compulsions include repeated cleaning, checking, counting, touching and hoarding of objects.

www.patient.co.uk/health/anxiety

Young people and anxiety

Anxiety is a condition that can affect anyone – it doesn't distinguish between age, background or social group. Even some of the most confident people you know may have suffered with anxiety. Recent research suggests that as many as one in six young people will experience an anxiety condition at some point in their lives, this means that up to five people in your class may be living with anxiety, whether that be OCD (obsessive compulsive disorder), social anxiety and shyness, exam stress, worry or panic attacks.

Many anxiety disorders begin in childhood and adolescence, and the average time a person waits to seek help for their condition (particularly for OCD and chronic worrying or GAD as it is known) is over ten years! That is a long time to be feeling anxious. You can save yourself a lot of stress by getting help sooner rather than later. At Anxiety UK we have trained volunteers who have lived with anxiety themselves. They are available Monday to Friday 9.30–5.30 and can help you decide what a good next step is for you. You don't have to suffer in silence.

There are also a number of services and resources that are designed for young people which you can access by becoming a member of Anxiety UK. If you do not wish to become a member, you can still access information and support through our e-mail information service and national helpline.

It can often be difficult to discuss how you feel with other people, especially if you think that no one else feels the same, or that they won't understand. You may feel that you don't fully understand what is happening to you, which can make it very hard to explain to others exactly what you are going through. Often, experiencing anxiety can leave you feeling tired, upset and frustrated. This can make you feel that you are unable to cope or that there is nothing that you can do to improve the situation.

Anxiety can affect us all in very different ways. Experiences of anxiety can vary greatly from person to person and no two people are the same. If you feel that any of the experiences or symptoms described on these pages apply to you, then we may be able to help.

First of all, anxiety is completely normal! It is something that we all experience to some level. Anxiety is useful to us as it tells us that something is dangerous and that we need to be careful. However, if anxiety gets out of control or stops you from doing everyday things, then this can lead to us feeling unhappy, upset and frustrated.

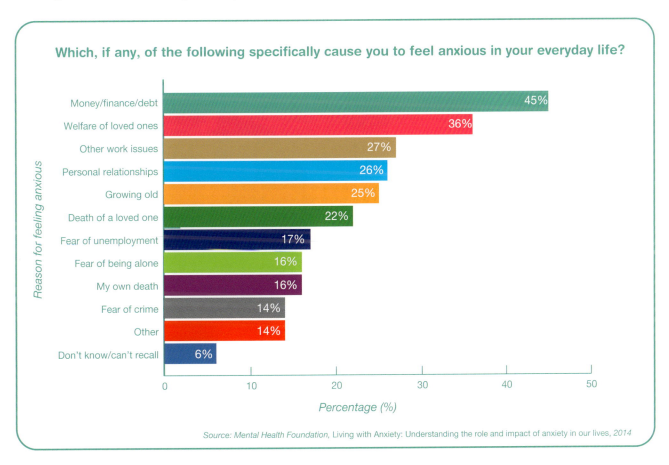

Which, if any, of the following specifically cause you to feel anxious in your everyday life?

Reason for feeling anxious

Reason	Percentage
Money/finance/debt	45%
Welfare of loved ones	36%
Other work issues	27%
Personal relationships	26%
Growing old	25%
Death of a loved one	22%
Fear of unemployment	17%
Fear of being alone	16%
My own death	16%
Fear of crime	14%
Other	14%
Don't know/can't recall	6%

Percentage (%)

Source: Mental Health Foundation, Living with Anxiety: Understanding the role and impact of anxiety in our lives, 2014

Here are some examples of how you might feel if you are anxious:

➤ Worried
➤ Upset
➤ Feeling sick
➤ Feeling shaky/dizzy
➤ Feeling like you might faint/pass out
➤ Thinking unpleasant thoughts
➤ Thinking that you might 'go crazy'.

When anxiety gets really strong, you might experience what we call a 'panic attack'. This is when your body is getting ready to fight, freeze or to run away from the situation that we are viewing as dangerous. This is known as the fight, flight or freeze response. Again, it can be quite scary to experience, although we know that it will not hurt you.

One of the ways to reduce the anxiety that you are feeling is to understand it better. By understanding how anxiety works, you can then understand why you feel that way and it will help you to break the vicious circle of anxiety that just makes things worse.

The 'fear of the fear' often makes us feel worse as we are literally on edge waiting for bad feelings to happen; we stop doing things that we link with the negative (bad) feelings or thoughts. This is called avoidance. The more that we avoid the thing that we link with feeling bad, the more we think of it as being dangerous.

This means that the next time we have to face the situation or event, our body tells us that it is dangerous and the fight, flight or freeze response kicks in. We feel that we either need to run away from the 'dangerous' thing, fight it or we feel that our body is frozen to the spot.

Either way, our body is not happy when we feel all of these horrible feelings and think horrible things. By understanding why we feel this way, we can then take away the 'scared' feeling because we know that it is just our body reacting to something that it thinks is scary, even though it is actually harmless. No-one ever died from having anxiety!

Getting help

The good news is that anxiety is treatable! This means that there are things that can be done to reduce feelings of anxiety. The first step is to speak to someone that you trust about how you are feeling. This could be a teacher, a parent, a relative or another adult that you trust. Talking to someone will reduce the pressure of anxiety and stress, it may also help you to realise that you are not alone in how you are feeling.

Talking to others

Often, because the anxious feelings and thoughts are so bad, we don't want to tell anyone how we feel as we believe that they might not understand or they might laugh at us. However, this is the best way to get help to change how you feel. Talking to someone about how you feel can help:

➤ Choose someone that you trust; for example, a parent/family member/teacher, etc.
➤ Tell them how you have been feeling and try to give them an example so that they understand clearly.
➤ If you are finding it hard to talk about this, try writing them a letter or showing them this article.
➤ Remember: It is okay to be upset and it is okay to ask for help.

Once you have spoken to someone, they will be able to get help for you.

You can also call Anxiety UK Helpline number: 08444 775 774 to talk to someone in complete confidence between 9.30 and 5.30, Monday to Friday.

www.anxietyuk.org.uk

Charity claims 20% of people regularly feel anxious

The Mental Health Foundation has published a report showing that almost one in five people feel anxious either a lot or all of the time.

Mike Brent, a Care UK recovery specialist, explains what can trigger feelings of anxiety and offers advice on how to deal with the condition, which is one of the most prevalent mental health problems in the UK.

Published last month, *Living with Anxiety – understanding the role and impact of anxiety in our lives* explores what can trigger feelings of anxiety, how it can be exacerbated by modern life and the impact it can have on people's lives. A survey conducted as part of the report also revealed that of the people affected by anxiety, two-thirds of them experience the emotion on a daily basis.

To help increase people's understanding of anxiety, this year's Mental Health Awareness Week (12–18 May) focused on the condition and its effect on the mental health and wellbeing of people throughout the country.

Care UK runs a range of services for people living with long-term mental health conditions. It offers expert support that is delivered using a person-centred approach designed to involve people in the planning and provision of their treatment. Mike Brent, clinical quality and audit manager at the independent health and social care provider, offers the following advice for people experiencing feelings of anxiety.

What is anxiety?

Anxiety is completely normal and everyone will experience it at some point in their lives, whether it is before attending a job interview or riding a roller coaster.

The purpose of anxiety is to prepare for danger by getting the body ready to defend itself or, in a modern day perspective, it helps you perform at your best. It's fair to say that without anxiety, the human race wouldn't survive.

However, anxiety can become a problem when the body reacts to no real danger. This can start to affect people on a day-to-day basis, which in turn affects how people cope with life's daily challenges.

When anxiety or worry feels extreme, it may be a sign of an anxiety disorder. For someone who has an anxiety disorder, getting proper care from a health professional is important. The following tips can help but if you feel things are getting out of control and you have difficulty functioning in daily life as you normally would, professional help is the best course of action.

Sometimes anxiety can cause a panic attack. If your heart rate rises or palms start to sweat the best thing is not to fight it. Stay where you are and simply feel the panic without trying to distract yourself. Placing the palm of your hand on your stomach and breathing slowly and deeply (no more than 12 breaths a minute) helps soothe the body. It may take up to an hour, but eventually the panic will go away on its own. The goal is to help the mind get used to coping with panic, which takes the worry of fear away.

Almost **one in five** people feel anxious all of the time or a lot of the time.

Only **one in 20** people never feel anxious.

Source: YouGov survey of 2,300 adults in Britain, Mental Health Week 2014

Tips for coping with anxiety

Become a relaxation expert

With our 24/7 society moving at ever increasing speed and with the advent of the Internet, smartphones and being constantly contactable via social media, people have forgotten the art of relaxation. Watching television or accessing the Internet is not true relaxation and depending on what you're watching, could make you more tense or anxious. The body needs true relaxation like deep breathing, tai chi or yoga that has a physical effect on the mind. A moment to close your eyes and imagine a place of safety and calm can enhance positive feelings and help you relax.

Back to basics

Get the right amount of sleep for your needs, not too much or too little. Eat a balanced diet and try to consume foods for long-term energy and not the short bursts that come from sugar or caffeine. Exercise sends oxygen to every cell in the body and will energise your body and mind. A good sleep and a balanced meal are often the best cures for anxiety.

Connect with others and talk about it

Spend time with friends and family. Doing things with people we like strengthens bonds and makes us feel supported and secure. Having fun makes us feel happy and less upset about things. Talking about problems helps us to feel understood and cared for and enhances the ability to cope. Likewise, sharing feelings of anxiety can take away their impact. If you can't talk to a friend, family member or partner there are many helplines that can assist.

Get outside

Getting away from the hustle and bustle of everyday life can help you feel more peaceful and grounded. Go somewhere you feel safe and can relax and enjoy your surroundings. The great outdoors can help to put things into perspective.

Think positive

Focus on thoughts and feelings that are good and positive. Allow yourself to daydream, wish and imagine the best that could happen.

Take time out

It's impossible to think clearly when you are anxious, with symptoms such as a racing heart, sweating palms, butterflies in your stomach and feeling nervous all being the result of adrenalin. You need to take time out to calm down physically. Walking, having a bath or having a cup of tea can help you physically calm down.

What's the worst that could happen?

Whatever is worrying you, it can help to think about the worst case scenario and plan for it, then, if the worst does happen, you can be ready. Fears tend to be much worse than the reality. For example, people sometimes feel very self-conscious when they blush in social situations and this makes you more anxious. This is a completely normal response and telling yourself this can help in banishing the anxiety.

Don't expect perfection

Unrealistic thoughts and goals can only set us up for anxiety. Life is full of stresses and strains and many people feel that life must be perfect. Bad days and setbacks will always happen and it is essential to remember that life can be messy and disorganised sometimes.

Reward yourself

Give yourself a treat when you have conquered your anxiety, reinforce your success with whatever makes you happy.

10 June 2014

www.careuk.com

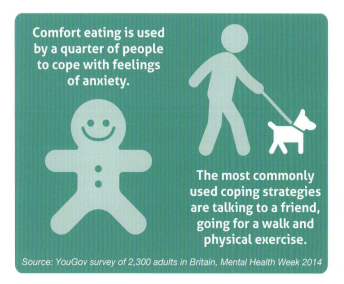

Comfort eating is used by a quarter of people to cope with feelings of anxiety.

The most commonly used coping strategies are talking to a friend, going for a walk and physical exercise.

Source: YouGov survey of 2,300 adults in Britain, Mental Health Week 2014

Anxiety: hospital admissions highest in women in their late 60s

Hospital admissions for anxiety increased with age and were highest among older women, new figures from the Health & Social Care Information Centre (HSCIC) show.

In the 12 months to November 2013 almost three out of ten anxiety admissions were women aged 60 and over (2,440 out of 8,720 or 28 per cent), with 65 to 69 the most common age group of female patient admissions (437, or eight per cent of all female admissions). The most common age group for male patient admissions was 45 to 49 (279, or 8.5 per cent of all male admissions).

This report, published 19 February 2014, also looks at hospital admissions for stress which were highest in girls aged 15 to 19 years (295) and men aged 40 to 44 years (343) and three-quarters of patients were under 50-years-old (74 per cent or 3,580 out of 4,840).

The pattern of admissions for anxiety or stress by age and gender was similar to the previous 12 months; however, total admissions fell by over two per cent for anxiety (from 8,930 to 8,720) and almost 14 per cent for stress (from 5,610 to 4,840).

The overall trend in admissions by age showed that anxiety admissions increased with age and stress

admissions amongst adults aged 45 years and above decreased with age.

The report focuses on a special topic which is part of a wider monthly publication of all NHS-commissioned provisional inpatient, outpatient and A&E activity in England. For all hospital admissions for anxiety or stress between December 2012 and November 2013:

➢ Women accounted for three in five anxiety admissions (62 per cent or 5,440) whereas more than half of stress admissions were men (55 per cent or 2,660) and this was similar to the previous 12 months (63 per cent and 55 per cent, respectively).

➢ Almost nine out of ten anxiety cases (89 per cent or 7,750) and eight out of ten stress cases (78 per cent or 3,760) were emergency admissions.

➢ One in five anxiety cases were diagnosed with high blood pressure (19 per cent or 1,660) and one in four stress admissions had a personal history of self-harm (25 per cent or 1,230).

➢ Merseyside Area Team had the highest rate of admissions for anxiety and stress (29.7 and 18.4 per 100,000 of the population) and Thames Valley Area Team had the lowest rate of admissions for both conditions (7.2 and 2.0 per 100,000, respectively).

Alan Perkins, CEO of the HSCIC, said: '[This] report shows striking age patterns in admissions for anxiety, and some interesting age and gender patterns for stress cases.

'Hospitals have dealt with fewer admissions for anxiety and stress compared to last year but the higher rates of anxiety in the older generation could be an area for concern.'

19 February 2014

www.hscic.gov.uk

20% take time off work due to stress

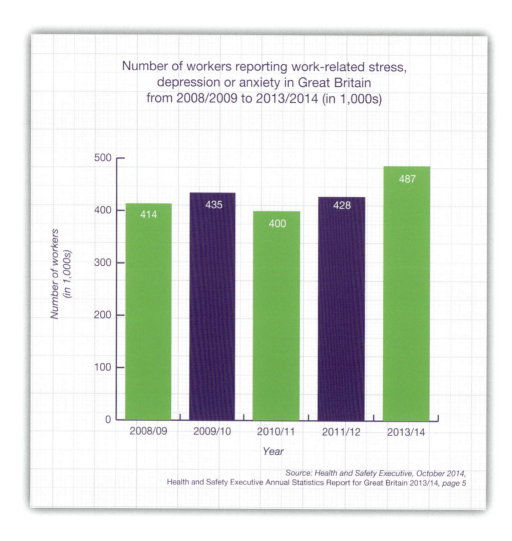

Number of workers reporting work-related stress, depression or anxiety in Great Britain from 2008/2009 to 2013/2014 (in 1,000s)

Number of workers (in 1,000s)

Year	Number
2008/09	414
2009/10	435
2010/11	400
2011/12	428
2013/14	487

Source: Health and Safety Executive, October 2014, Health and Safety Executive Annual Statistics Report for Great Britain 2013/14, page 5

By Robert Crawford

One in five (20%) respondents have taken time off work due to a stress-related illness in the past 12 months, according to research by MetLife Employee Benefits.

This research, which surveyed 2,134 respondents aged 18 and above, found that one in ten respondents have taken more than six days off work due to stress.

The research found stress was a bigger cause of absence in the past year than sports-related injuries (10%) and hangovers or other alcohol-related issues (8%).

The research also found that nearly two-thirds (63%) of respondents would welcome help and advice from their employer on how to improve their health and wellbeing.

Currently, 61% of respondents receive some form of health and wellness support at work, with health advice being the most common provision, offered to 37%.

Only 13% are provided with group income protection policies.

Tom Gaynor, employee benefits director at MetLife, said: 'Stress is a major issue with one in five employees having to take time off work in the past year.

'It is clear that staff would welcome more support and help from employers on health and wellness in the workplace, and it is also clear that employers have recognised the need to provide support.

'There is a genuine benefit for both employers and employees in promoting good health at work.

'Helping staff to be healthier cuts the cost of absence for employers and enables employees to avoid illness where possible and to recover faster.'

11 April 2014

www.employeebenefits.co.uk

Work stress may be causing Brits to drink, smoke and do less exercise, study finds

Stress caused by work may be having a serious negative impact on the nation's health. That's according to a new study that revealed many people feel work pressures make them drink and smoke more, put on weight and do less exercise.

A survey of almost 1,400 workers revealed that almost a third believed work-related stress could lead to high blood pressure, while one in five feared it could cause a heart attack.

The British Heart Foundation (BHF) urged employers to encourage workers to spend at least ten minutes a day improving their lifestyle.

Lisa Young, Project Manager for the BHF's Health at Work programme, said: 'This survey is a stark reminder of just what happens when we don't take our health at work seriously enough.

'Millions of people say they are smoking more, exercising less and putting on weight because they're not considering the impact their job is having on their health and wellbeing.

'Behaviours like these can be extremely damaging, not just to your heart health but also to businesses. From working with over 9,500 organisations we know that the pay-offs of making health at work a top businesses priority are too great to ignore.'

A third of those polled said they had put on weight because of work, half ate more unhealthily, a quarter drink more and 43% believe work has caused them to exercise less.

TUC general secretary Frances O'Grady said: 'The BHF report is a shocking indictment of the modern world of work.

'Long hours, the insecurity of jobs on zero-hours contracts and the stress associated with them are all taking a toll on people's health.

'The report's findings show just how bad some workplaces have become. However, the answer is not just for employers to encourage their staff to change their lifestyle – it is for employers to improve working conditions, provide secure jobs and treat their workers like human beings rather than machines.'

12 February 2015

The above information is reprinted with kind permission from the Press Association. © Press Association 2015

www.pressassociation.com

Four in every ten employed people experience anxiety about their work.

Source: YouGov survey of 2,300 adults in Britain, Mental Health Week 2014

Mini glossary

Indictment – *something which shows that a situation or system is bad and deserves disapproval.*

Zero-hour contract – *a work contract where the employer is not required to offer a minimum number of working hours (this means no guarantee of work), or for workers to accept it. This allows workers to be flexible with their hours, but they might be expected to be on call and work with very little notice or compensation. Sick pay is often not included, but holiday pay can be.*

Activities

Brainstorm

1. What is stress?

2. What is anxiety?

3. How are stress and anxiety different?

Oral activity

4. As a class, make a list of the most common causes of stress. Select one item from your list and brainstorm the issue with a partner. How many people in the UK suffer from stress as a result of this problem? How could it be avoided? What are the most effective solutions to stress arising from this issue?

Research activities

5. Do some research about post-traumatic stress in relation to the military. When did people first start recognising this as a condition? What kind of treatments are available? Write some notes and feedback to your class.

6. Do you think modern life is more stressful than life in the UK 50 years ago? Speak to people you know who were young adults during the 1950s and 60s. Do they feel life was more or less stressful at that time compared to young people's lives today?

Written activity

7. Do you ever feel stressed? Keep a stress diary for a fortnight, recording every time you felt stressed, what caused it and how you reacted. Review your diary: is there anything you could change in your life to avoid stress?

Moral dilemma

8. Consider our attitude to stress in the western world. Is stress also an issue in developing countries? Discuss with a partner.

Design activities

9. Design a poster that will help people recognise the symptoms of anxiety.

10. Design a website that will give parents information about anxiety in young people. Think about the kind of information they might need (e.g. exam stress) and give your site a name and logo.

Mental health costs 'astounding' – and on rise

Around 70 million working days were lost last year because of mental health and England's Chief Medical Officer says the NHS and employers need to do more to help support sufferers at work.

Stress and depression should be treated in the same way as physical health, said Professor Dame Sally Davies, who is calling for a radical rethink in the way it is treated. She has called for funding for these services to be protected, amid warnings that they are being cut, and suggested implementing waiting time targets for treatment.

Dame Sally said the number of working days lost due to stress, depression and anxiety has increased by 24 per cent since 2009, costing an estimated £100 billion and that the number lost due to serious mental illness has doubled.

Providing a supportive working environment for people with mental health illnesses – for example, allowing more flexible working hours, or part-time working post-illness – could be a key way to prevent sufferers from having to take time off work, she added. An estimated 60 to 70 per cent of people with common mental health disorders were in full-time work.

In her annual report on the mental health of people in England, Dame Sally also said it was striking that three quarters of people with diagnosable mental illness have no treatment at all.

'Treatment gap'

'The costs of mental illness to the economy are astounding,' she said. 'Through this report, I urge commissioners and decision-makers to treat mental health more like physical health.

'The World Health Organization model of mental health promotion, mental illness prevention and treatment and rehabilitation should be adopted in public mental health in England.

'Anyone with mental illness deserves good quality support at the right time. One of the stark issues highlighted in this report is that 60 to 70 per cent of people

with common mental disorders such as depression and anxiety are in work, so it is crucial that we take action to help those people stay in employment to benefit their own health as well as the economy.'

Dr Peter Carter, chief executive and general secretary of the Royal College of Nursing, said: 'The treatment gap for people with mental health problems can no longer be ignored. Not only are people with mental health problems in need of better support for their mental health conditions, but there is an unacceptable and preventable level of correlation with physical ill health.'

9 September 2014

www.channel4.com

Ten stress busters

What's making you stressed?

If you're stressed, whether by your job or by something more personal, the first step to feeling better is to identify the cause.

The most unhelpful thing you can do is turn to something unhealthy to help you cope, such as smoking or drinking.

'In life, there's always a solution to a problem,' says Professor Cary Cooper, an occupational health expert at the University of Lancaster. 'Not taking control of the situation and doing nothing will only make your problems worse.'

He says the keys to good stress management are building emotional strength, being in control of your situation, having a good social network and adopting a positive outlook.

What you can do to address stress

These are Professor Cooper's top ten stress-busting suggestions:

Be active

If you have a stress-related problem, physical activity can get you in the right state of mind to be able to identify the causes of your stress and find a solution. 'To deal with stress effectively, you need to feel robust and you need to feel strong mentally. Exercise does that,' says Cooper.

Exercise won't make your stress disappear, but it will reduce some of the emotional intensity that you're feeling, clearing your thoughts and enabling you to deal with your problems more calmly.

Take control

There's a solution to any problem. 'If you remain passive, thinking, 'I can't do anything about my problem', your stress will get worse,' says Professor Cooper. 'That feeling of loss of control is one of the main causes of stress and lack of wellbeing.'

The act of taking control is in itself empowering, and it's a crucial part of finding a solution that satisfies you and not someone else. Read tips about how to manage your time.

Connect with people

A problem shared is a problem halved. A good support network of colleagues, friends and family can ease your work troubles and help you see things in a different way.

'If you don't connect with people, you won't have support to turn to when you need help,' says Professor Cooper. The activities we do with friends help us relax and we often have a good laugh with them, which is an excellent stress reliever.

'Talking things through with a friend will also help you find solutions to your problems,' says Professor Cooper.

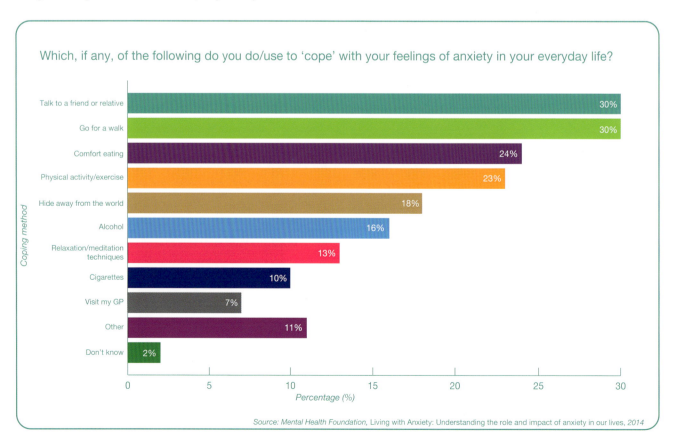

Which, if any, of the following do you do/use to 'cope' with your feelings of anxiety in your everyday life?

Coping method	Percentage (%)
Talk to a friend or relative	30%
Go for a walk	30%
Comfort eating	24%
Physical activity/exercise	23%
Hide away from the world	18%
Alcohol	16%
Relaxation/meditation techniques	13%
Cigarettes	10%
Visit my GP	7%
Other	11%
Don't know	2%

Source: Mental Health Foundation, Living with Anxiety: Understanding the role and impact of anxiety in our lives, 2014

Have some 'me time'

The UK workforce works the longest hours in Europe. The extra hours in the workplace mean that people aren't spending enough time doing things that they really enjoy. 'We all need to take some time for socialising, relaxation or exercise,' says Professor Cooper.

He recommends setting aside a couple of nights a week for some quality 'me time' away from work. 'By earmarking those two days, it means you won't be tempted to work overtime on those days,' he says.

Challenge yourself

Setting yourself goals and challenges, whether at work or outside, such as learning a new language or a new sport, helps to build confidence. That in turn will help you deal with stress.

'By constantly challenging yourself you're being proactive and taking charge of your life,' says Professor Cooper. 'By continuing to learn, you become more emotionally resilient as a person. It arms you with knowledge and makes you want to do things rather than be passive, such as watching TV all the time.'

Avoid unhealthy habits

Don't rely on alcohol, smoking and caffeine as your ways of coping. 'Men more than women are likely to do this. We call this avoidance behaviour,' says Professor Cooper. 'Women are better at seeking support from their social circle.'

Over the long term, these crutches won't solve your problems. They'll just create new ones. 'It's like putting your head in the sand,' says Professor Cooper. 'It might provide temporary relief but it won't make the problems disappear. You need to tackle the cause of your stress.'

Help other people

Cooper says evidence shows that people who help others, through activities such as volunteering or community work, become more resilient. 'Helping people who are often in situations worse than yours will help you put your problems into perspective,' says Professor Cooper. 'The more you give, the more resilient and happy you feel.'

If you don't have time to volunteer, try to do someone a favour every day. It can be something as small as helping someone to cross the road or going on a coffee run for colleagues. Favours cost nothing to do, and you'll feel better.

Work smarter, not harder

Good time management means quality work rather than quantity. Our long-hours culture is a well-known cause of workplace illness. 'You have to get a work-life balance that suits you,' says Professor Cooper.

Working smarter means prioritising your work, concentrating on the tasks that will make a real difference to your work. 'Leave the least important tasks to last,' says Cooper. 'Accept that your in-tray will always be full. Don't expect it to be empty at the end of the day.'

Be positive

Look for the positives in life, and things for which you're grateful. Write down three things at the end of every day which went well or for which you're grateful.

'People don't always appreciate what they have,' says Professor Cooper. 'Try to be glass half full instead of glass half empty,' he says.

This requires a shift in perspective for those who are more naturally pessimistic.

'It can be done,' he says. 'By making a conscious effort you can train yourself to be more positive about life. Problems are often a question of perspective. If you change your perspective, you may see your situation from a more positive point of view.'

Accept the things you can't change

Changing a difficult situation isn't always possible. If this proves to be the case, recognise and accept things as they are and concentrate on everything that you do have control over.

'If your company is going under and is making redundancies, there's nothing you can do about it,' says Professor Cooper. 'There's no point fighting it. In such a situation, you need to focus on the things that you can control, such as looking for a new job.'

6 January 2014

www.nhs.uk

Mini glossary

Robust – *strong, tough.*

How colouring books are helping adults beat stress and anxiety

By Rachel Moss

Colouring books for adults are outselling cookery books in France, and now they appear to be taking over bookshelves in the UK, too. But why?

While drawing between the lines was once reserved for children, colouring is now being used as a form of alternative therapy to help adults relieve stress and anxiety.

According to the Mental Health Foundation, 59% of adults in Britain say they are more stressed today than they were five years ago. It's no wonder we're looking for a way to feel calm.

But is grabbing the crayons the answer?

'Colouring is a great way to introduce yourself to the concept of mindfulness,' Tiddy Rowan, author of *The Little Book Of Mindfulness* and *Colour Yourself Calm* tells HuffPost UK Lifestyle.

'One gets so engrossed in colouring, it's an extraordinary activity – in fact, if you watch children playing with crayons you can see just how absorbing it is.'

Tiddy believes colouring can make mindfulness more accessible to stressed adults as the action requires the mind to focus on the present moment.

'Sometimes when you're trying to remember a fact but you can't think of the answer, it will only come to you later when you're doing something else entirely. Colouring can help us to experience clarity of the mind more easily,' she adds.

Co-illustrator of *The Creative Therapy Colouring Book* Richard Merritt agrees that colouring can provide a much needed distraction from stress, and says the experience can transport us back to easier, childhood days.

'When you're colouring, you're not really thinking about anything else. In that moment – when you're sitting down with a traditional piece of paper and some pens, no apps, no noise – you almost go back to being a kid again. Colouring provides a bit of escapism.

'If you put a piece of paper and a crayon in front of a child, they'll start drawing, but I think as an adult you lose that spontaneity,' he says.

Facebook groups have been set up in response to the colouring book trend, with women (the gender predominantly taking part in the activity) coming together and sharing their stories online.

Cynthia Riviere, who administrates a Facebook group of more than 1,000 colouring book fans, spends more than an hour a day filling in the gaps of her favourite books.

She told *The Telegraph*: 'I realised that colouring makes my headaches go away. I concentrate, my breathing slows down and I move into a deep calm.'

This sense of calm that Cynthia and may others experience when colouring may be down to the simplicity of the activity. Recent studies have shown that the majority of adults feel like they are constantly looking at a screen, and crave a slower pace life.

Both Richard and Tiddy believe the growing interest in mindfulness and alternative therapy stems from our dissatisfaction with modern culture.

'We are constantly bombarded with technology, you can download apps to your phone in a few seconds and it's too much for us to take in. Colouring allows us to go back to a slower pace and I think people appreciate that,' Richard says.

According to Tiddy, colouring can help us to reconnect with ourselves which in turn can help us reach out to those around us.

'We're reaching out to each other on social media, but that isn't satisfying. We connect to others through a screen today, but mindfulness encourages us to live in the present moment and connect to those physically around us.

'By making a few simple lifestyle changes, mindfulness is something you can begin to practice immediately – it doesn't require extensive study, expensive classes or a big time commitment.

'The interesting thing about mindfulness is that it's got no allegiance to any spiritual or religious beliefs, it's about the self,' Tiddy says. 'I think that's perhaps key to the popularity of these colouring books.'

7 October 2014

www.huffingtonpost.co.uk

Why is it important to breathe properly to help anxiety?

We are going to look at hyperventilating (or over-breathing) because when we are anxious we tend to over-breathe. Sometimes this can develop into a bad habit which we end up doing all the time without being aware of it.

About 60% of panic attacks are accompanied by hyperventilation and many people suffering from anxiety over-breathe even when they think they are relaxed.

The most important thing to understand about hyperventilation, or over breathing, is that although we feel as if we don't have enough oxygen in our body, actually the opposite is true: with hyperventilation the body has too much oxygen. To use this oxygen your body needs a certain amount of carbon dioxide.

When we hyperventilate we do not give the body long enough to retain carbon dioxide and so the body cannot use the oxygen it has. This gives a feeling that there isn't enough air in the body, when actually there is too much – we are in the cycle of a chemical imbalance. The problem is that the shortage of carbon dioxide causes many problems. Even though carbon dioxide is a waste gas, we do need it in certain parts of the body, especially the brain. Although this chemical imbalance can be extremely unpleasant it will not harm anyone. With the help of special breathing techniques, this can restore the correct balance and give a person control over anxiety. Regular relaxation and correct breathing will stop the production of stress hormones (cortisol, non-adrenalin and adrenalin).

Control centre

We have a control centre at the base of our brain which measures the levels of carbon dioxide in the blood and keeps our breathing balanced. It sends a message to our body on how we should breathe. When we are breathing incorrectly because carbon dioxide levels get low the breathing control centre goes down a notch and when we start to breathe normally it goes back to its original position. However, if we continue to breathe incorrectly, the breathing control centre level stays where it is and encourages us to breathe faster – this is when we can develop bad breathing habits and are not aware that this can contribute to the symptoms of anxiety. If anxiety and stress become a bad habit the body becomes more alert and prone to panic.

Symptoms that may be experienced

- Light headedness
- Giddiness
- Dizziness
- Shortness of breath
- Heart palpitation
- Numbness
- Chest pains
- Dry mouth
- Clammy hands
- Difficulty in swallowing
- Sweating
- Weakness
- Fatigue.

It takes up a lot more energy when we are breathing incorrectly, so this can make us feel very tired.

If you find that your breathing pattern is irregular or uncomfortable a lot of the time, the best way to reset it is by exercising. Start off gradually and check with your doctor if you are not used to exercise.

Bad breathing restricts blood flow to the brain and affects nerve cells. This can cause dizziness and tingling. Low carbon dioxide levels affect the nervous system. This puts the body on alert. Continued bad breathing causes exhaustion, tiredness and depression. Oxygen levels are lower in the brain and this means we cannot concentrate. The drop in oxygen levels stimulates the breathing control centre which then increases the breathing rate to compensate and this then encourages hyperventilation. The brain resets and an over-breathing habit may be formed. We may not even be aware of what has happened.

Practising breathing techniques will stimulate the part of the nervous system responsible for relaxation and will help to calm the body down. It may take a few minutes but the body will respond regardless of what the mind is thinking. Doing this regularly with a relaxation CD will cause general anxiety levels to come down. With practice, we want to try and aim to keep anxiety at a lower base line of arousal as this then stops the body becoming anxious at the slightest thing and makes it harder to get stressed. Regular relaxation and the breathing technique start to stop the production of stress hormones in the body so it becomes harder to panic.

Try this test

Let us try and see where you are breathing from, the chest or the tummy. Put one hand below your collar bone and one on your diaphragm, which is just below your rib cage, and breathe how you would normally would. Are you breathing from the chest are or you breathing correctly from your diaphragm?

Take a deep breath through the mouth and see how that feels. Can you feel cold air hitting the back of the throat? That in fact will make us breathe quicker, which will increase anxiety and the symptoms we experience.

Now breathe through the nose with the mouth shut. How does that feel? The air is warm and also filtered of germs so it is much healthier.

Diaphragm

The diaphragm is a sheet of muscle shaped like an umbrella that goes up and down as we breathe. It flattens down to expand the lungs and that is why the stomach expands as we breathe in. It draws in oxygen-rich air with little effort. As the diaphragm relaxes the dome shape is restored and carbon dioxide-rich air is gently exhaled. The diaphragm is tailor made to fit your body and its sole purpose is to supply the right amount of air to the lungs during rest and normal activity.

Have you ever looked at babies when they are breathing? You can hardly see their body moving and that is because they are breathing from the diaphragm. If you have pets, cats and dogs for example, they just flop, drop and again breathe very steady and rhythmic. This is a perfect example of breathing from the diaphragm.

Breathing techniques

The best way to start is to lie on a bed and place your hands gently on your stomach (where the diaphragm is) with your fingertips touching and as you breathe in your fingertips should come apart and as you breathe out they come back together again.

Next you might want to try placing one hand gently on your tummy, just below your rib cage, and as you breathe in push your tummy gently up and as you breathe out your tummy should gently come down again. The aim is to breathe in a steady rhythm, with no pause between the in and out breaths (not deep breathing). Try and concentrate just on your breath going in and out.

Breathe in through the nose with the mouth closed (count to four) and breathe out again through the nose, keeping the mouth closed (count to four). Feel your stomach expand as you breathe in, inflate it like a balloon, and as you breathe out allow your stomach to deflate. Try and just concentrate on your breath going in and out – aim for eight to ten breathes a minute (breathing in and out counts as one breath). What this does is restore the

Source: Coping with Shortness of Breath: Controlling Stress, University of Minnesota Masonic Children's Hospital, 2015.

chemical imbalance and it will calm the mind and body down, which will reduce symptoms of anxiety.

As you get used to doing this breathing technique, you can start practising in different places, like practise your breathing sitting in a chair, then perhaps when washing up or standing in a queue in the supermarket – eventually you can learn to do this way of breathing anywhere in your anxious situations. You do have to practise this regularly because your body is probably not used to breathing this way and needs time to adjust.

Problems

Resist the temptation to take in huge gulps of air. If we breathe in big, we are going to breathe out big too which further depletes carbon dioxide levels.

If a person feels dizzy it means they are still breathing big rather than deep breathing. To overcome this, cup both hands over the mouth and nose and re-breathe carbon dioxide-rich air for five of six breathes, then rest. Repeat this until the dizziness has gone.

We may have the urge to yawn, sigh or gulp in air. It may seem overwhelming and very uncomfortable, but this is a sign of progress and shows that the breathing is beginning to work. The body is trying to make you breathe faster, but with practice the breathing centre will adjust and your body will get used to the new way of breathing. The diaphragm may struggle at first, especially if it has been out of action for a while. Like any other group of muscles that have not been used, the diaphragm may need strengthening. Be patient, with practice it will work better.

Set your alarm five minutes earlier in the morning and start the day with good breathing practice. Check the chest area regularly through the day to correct your breathing, and then forget it. It is important not to worry about breathing too much and let it come naturally. As you become accustomed to this new way of breathing there will be less need to check the chest. During stressful times, however, it pays to check the breathing rate and patterns – concentrating on breathing helps to calm down anxiety.

4 August 2014

www.nopanic.org.uk

Attitudes to
Counselling & Psychotherapy
Key findings of our 2014 Survey

bacp
British Association for
Counselling & Psychotherapy

Background

Our latest survey explores the British public's attitudes to counselling and psychotherapy, and highlights changes in attitudes since our previous surveys in 2004 and 2010.

2084 adults from across the UK completed this survey, which was conducted by Ipsos MORI in March 2014.

Have you ever consulted a counsellor or psychotherapist?

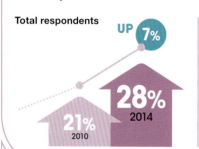

Total respondents

UP **7%**

28% 2014

21% 2010

Gender split

32% **23%**

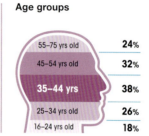

Age groups

55–75 yrs old	**24%**
45–54 yrs old	**32%**
35–44 yrs	**38%**
25–34 yrs old	**26%**
16–24 yrs old	**18%**

54% of people say that a family member, friend, work colleague or themselves **have consulted a counsellor or psychotherapist**

54%

Seeking help

Percentage of people who said they'd know where to seek help if they had, or experienced:

WORKPLACE STRESS	**45%**
GAMBLING ADDICTION	**52%**
ANXIETY	**61%**
DEPRESSION	**71%**

People would seek help from a variety of different sources:

64% GP

41% Counsellor or psychotherapist

44% Consult a family member

30% Telephone helpline

27% Contact an advice agency/charity

39% Look online

47% Self-help books or pamphlets

76% of people say they'd prefer to speak to a counsellor face to face, with only **9%** saying they'd prefer to speak online

76% **9%**

SELF-HARM PORNOGRAPHY SEX ADDICTION

14% **73%**

That said, with regards to problems relating to self-harm, pornography or sex addiction, **14%** of people say they'd rather speak online. **73%** of these said they'd prefer to speak online as it would make them feel more anonymous

---

Acceptance

In 2004, **60%** of people agreed that "people today spend too much time dwelling on their emotional difficulties," in 2014 this has dropped to **39%**

60% 2004

39% 2014

64%

64% of people think that counselling should be available to all school children in schools

69%

69% of people think that the world would be a better place if people talked about their feelings more

About BACP

BACP is a professional body and a registered charity that sets standards for therapeutic practice and provides information for therapists, clients of therapy, and the public.

We have over 40,000 members, working within a range of settings, including the NHS, schools and universities, workplaces and private practice, as well as third sector environments including voluntary, community and pastoral settings.

Workplace & coaching

48% of people say they feel stressed more regularly these days than they did five years ago

STRESS **48%**

32% of people say their job causes them more stress than anything else in their life.

In London this figure is higher, with **37%** saying their job causes them the most stress

32%

37%

Have you ever taken part in a coaching session?

YES 16%

18% **14%**

53% YES

53% of people say they would accept a free coaching session offered by their employer

37% of people would be more likely to accept the offer of coaching by an employer than counselling, compared to **17%** who would chose counselling over coaching

37% COACHING **17%** COUNSELLING

BACP Media

We are committed to providing prompt responses to media enquiries, drawing on our extensive member network of experts and spokespeople.

For all media enquiries, call our media team on 01455 883342, or email media@bacp.co.uk.

bacp

British Association for
Counselling & Psychotherapy

Company limited by guarantee 2175320
Registered in England & Wales.
Registered Charity 298361

'I had three or four flashbacks a day'

In some unique cases, the vivid recollection of a trauma can cause distress many years after the incident. Andy, an ex-fire officer, describes his experience of post-traumatic stress disorder (PTSD) and how the right treatment has helped him to move on.

'The event that caused my trauma happened 20 years ago when I was a fire officer. I was in charge of an appliance at a house fire where three people had died. It was my job to take their remains out of the house.

'A few days later I became distressed and started crying and feeling upset. This strong reaction came as a shock, but I said nothing at the time. I think this was partly because I didn't want to share my emotions with anybody.

'My feelings and thoughts continued to bother me for a few weeks. After a while I decided that, because of my job, being like this was no good and I had to put these emotions to one side.

'These early responses to the trauma indicated the huge wave of feelings and sensations that would come back 17 years later in a way I couldn't ignore.

'I was still a firefighter. I kept remembering that terrible event and the feelings it left me with, but I tried not to think about it. A few days later my colleagues and I were at another house fire. It was similar to the one in which the family had died. Suddenly, I felt as if I wasn't there. My mind was totally occupied in a flashback of the original incident. One of my colleagues had to step in and take over from me.

'From then on I started to become distressed for no real reason. Everything seemed emotional, and I felt raw and exposed. I got easily frustrated, which made me short-tempered and angry.

'When the distress was at its worst, I had three or four flashbacks a day. I would sweat and become very nervous as I remembered the events 20 years ago. All the smells were there, and I even felt the heat of the fire moving across my face. People who saw me say that I sometimes walked about and mouthed words, but I was completely detached from my surroundings.

'That was when it became obvious that I couldn't go on. After some time, I had a course of trauma-focused cognitive behavioural therapy with a PTSD charity called ASSIST. They helped me to understand that I had experienced something abnormal, that none of it was my fault, and that there was nothing wrong or crazy about my emotional responses.

'Talking about the fire was uncomfortable at times, but it helped me to process my memories so that they stopped reappearing as flashbacks. They have gone now, and I am able to get on with my life.'

24 September 2013

www.nhs.uk

Good stress

By Christina Hughes

Did you know that not all stress is necessarily bad? While everyone reacts to stress and handles it in different ways – some people can thrive on it whereas some people may find it difficult to cope – there are potential benefits to experiencing 'good stress'. In the short-term good stress can:

➤ **Help increase immunity** – a temporary defensive boost which helps the body prepare for potential injuries or infection.

➤ **Boost your brainpower** – concentration and productivity can increase when you're under the pressure of stress and even enhance your memory.

➤ **Motivate you to success** – if there is a deadline looming, stress can help you to effectively tackle the task by letting you see that situation as a challenge to beat, rather than a wall and being overwhelmed by it.

Of course, even too much good stress is unhealthy. In the short-term, stress can give you the energy to perform your best, such as during a presentation or at a sporting event. However, too much stress or long-term stress can drain you physically and emotionally (e.g. you can potentially experience anxiety and health problems).

It is important to find a nice balance of good stress. Understanding your stress level is key, as recognising and managing your stress will help you lead a happy and healthy life.

8 September 2015

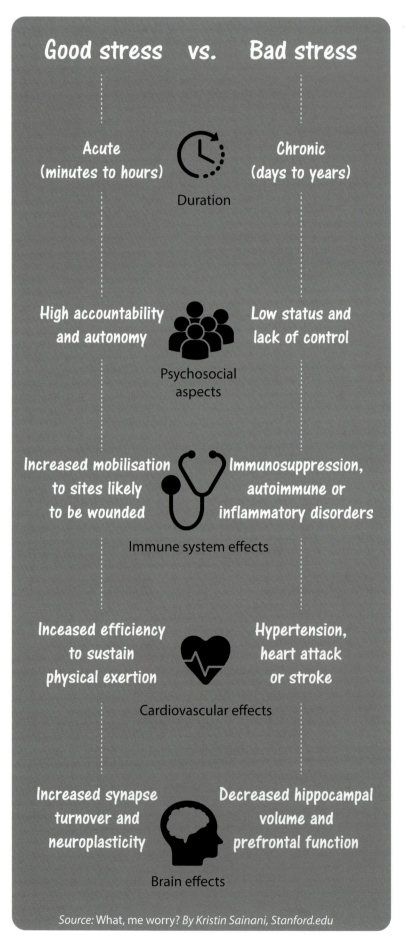

Good stress vs. Bad stress

Acute (minutes to hours) — Chronic (days to years)
Duration

High accountability and autonomy — Low status and lack of control
Psychosocial aspects

Increased mobilisation to sites likely to be wounded — Immunosuppression, autoimmune or inflammatory disorders
Immune system effects

Inceased efficiency to sustain physical exertion — Hypertension, heart attack or stroke
Cardiovascular effects

Increased synapse turnover and neuroplasticity — Decreased hippocampal volume and prefrontal function
Brain effects

Source: What, me worry? By Kristin Sainani, Stanford.edu

Activities

Brainstorm

1. What kind of things do people do to cope with stress and anxiety?

2. Is there such a thing as 'good stress'?

Oral activities

3. In pairs, role play one of the following situations:

   - An employee telling their line manager that they are suffering from work-related stress, and the line manager's response.

   - A student telling their friend that they are feeling lonely and anxious, and the friend's advice.

4. 'We all get stressed from time to time, but most people manage to deal with it without counselling or treatment. People suffering from stress should stop being self-indulgent and pull themselves together.' Do you think this view is too harsh or do you think it has a point? Discuss your views with a partner.

Research activities

5. Do some research to find out more about the idea of good stress verses bad stress. Make some notes and discuss your findings with your class.

6. Find out more about cognitive behavioural therapy (CBT). What does this treatment involve and how can it help people to deal with stress and anxiety symptoms?

Written activity

7. Write a step-by-step guide on how to breathe properly and how it can help with anxiety. Feel free to include diagrams and illustrations.

Moral dilemma

8. Consider the following statement: 'Stress should be treated the same way as physical health.' Do you agree or disagree? Why?

Design activity

9. Create a booklet to help students manage stress. Provide broad information on how to cope with stress, including relaxation techniques, tips on nutrition and anything else you think your readers would find helpful – you could even include some stress-busting meal ideas or suggest a relaxation playlist! Keep the tone light and fun and include illustrations.

Key facts

➤ If you have a pre-existing health condition, stress may cause it to worsen or flare-up. For example, conditions such as migraine, eczema, asthma, irritable bowel syndrome or psoriasis can all be made worse by stress. (page 1)

➤ Exercise can be effective at relieving stress and is good for your wellbeing... The recommended healthy level of physical activity is 150 minutes (two-and-a-half-hours) of moderate exercise per week. (page 2)

➤ The diagnosis 'PTSD' was first used by veterans of the Vietnam War, but the problem has existed for a lot longer and has had a variety of names, including: shell shock, soldier's heart, battle fatigue, combat stress and post-traumatic stress syndrome (PTSS). (page 3)

➤ About one in 20 people have an anxiety disorder at any one time. (page 7)

➤ Panic attacks [can] usually last five to ten minutes, but sometimes they come in waves for up to two hours. (page 8)

➤ Almost one in five people feel anxious all of the time or a lot of the time. (page 11)

➤ Only one in 20 people never feel anxious. (page 11)

➤ Comfort eating is used by a quarter of people to cope with feelings of anxiety. (page 12)

➤ The most commonly used coping strategies are talking to a friend, going for a walk and physical exercise. (page 12)

➤ In the 12 months to November 2013, 65 to 69 was the most common age group of female patient admissions for anxiety (437, or eight per cent of all female admissions). The most common age group for male patient admissions was 45 to 49 (279, or 8.5 per cent of all male admissions). (page 13)

➤ One in five (20%) respondents have taken time off work due to a stress-related illness in the past 12 months, according to research by MetLife Employee Benefits... – stress was a bigger cause of absence in the past year than sports-related injuries (10%) and hangovers or other alcohol-related issues (8%). (page 14)

➤ Four in every ten employed people experience anxiety about their work. (page 15)

➤ Dame Sally said the number of working days lost due to stress, depression and anxiety has increased by 24 per cent since 2009, costing an estimated £100 billion. (page 17)

➤ About 60% of panic attacks are accompanied by hyperventilation and many people suffering from anxiety over-breathe even when they think they are relaxed. (page 21)

➤ The British Association for Counselling & Psychotherapy 2014 survey found that 28% of respondents have consulted a counsellor or psychotherapist (up from 21% in 2010). Of those who had have consulted a counsellor or psychotherapist, 32% were female and 23% were male. (page 24)

Glossary

Agoraphobia – Fear of public places.

Angst – A feeling of anxiety or apprehension.

Anxiety – Feeling nervous, worried or distressed, sometimes a point where the person feels so overwhelmed that they fir everyday life very difficult to handle.

Cognitive behavioural therapy (CBT) – A psychological treatme which assumes that behavioural and emotional reactions a learned over a long period. A cognitive therapist will seek identify the source of emotional problems and develop techniqu to overcome them.

Depression – Someone is said to be significantly depressed, suffering from depression, when feelings of sadness or misery dor go away quickly and are so bad that they interfere with everyda life. Symptoms can also include low self-esteem and a lack motivation. Depression can be triggered by a traumatic/difficu event (reactive depression), but not always (e.g. endogenou depression).

Fight or flight response – Also called the stress response, th refers to a physical reaction the body encounters when face with something it perceives to be a threat. The nervous system primed, preparing the body to either fight the threat or run awa from it. In the past, this response would have helped human bein to survive threats such as predatory animals. While this no long applies to our modern lifestyles, our bodies will still react with tł fight-or-flight response to any perceived threat – an approachir deadline, for example – causing many of the negative sympton of stress.

Generalised anxiety disorder (GAD) – Someone with GAD has a l of anxiety (feeling fearful, worried and tense) on most days, ar not just in specific situations, and the condition persists long-terr Some of the physical symptoms of anxiety come and go. Someor with this high level of 'background anxiety' may also have pan attacks and some phobias.

Mindfulness – Mind-body based training that uses meditatio breathing and yoga techniques to help you focus on your though and feelings. Mindfulness helps you manage your thoughts ar feelings better, instead of being overwhelmed by them.

Panic attack – A panic attack is a severe attack of anxiety and fe which occurs suddenly, often without warning, and for no appare reason. Symptoms can include palpitations, sweating, tremblin nausea and hyperventilation. At least one in ten people hav occasional panic attacks. They tend to occur most in young adult

Post-traumatic stress disorder (PTSD) – PTSD is a psychologic reaction to a highly traumatic event. It has been known by differe names at different times in history: during the First World Wa for example, soldiers suffering from PTSD were said to have 'she shock'.

Social anxiety disorder – Fear of social situations.

Stress – Stress is the feeling of being under pressure. A little bit pressure can be a good thing, helping to motivate you: however, tc much pressure or prolonged pressure can lead to stress, which unhealthy for the mind and body and can cause symptoms such a lack of sleep, loss of appetite and difficulty concentrating.

Work-life balance – The concept of achieving a healthy baland between your career/work commitments and your home-life (famil friends, socialising, leisure activities, etc.).